AUDREY WOOD

Illustrated by
DON WOOD

THE NAPPING HOUSE

HARCOURT BRACE & COMPANY

San Diego   New York   London

Text copyright © 1984 by Audrey Wood
Illustrations copyright © 1984 by Don Wood

Library of Congress Cataloging-in-Publication Data
Wood, Audrey.
The napping house.
Summary: In this cumulative tale, a wakeful flea atop a number
of sleeping creatures causes a commotion, with just one bite.
[1. Sleep — Fiction. 2. Fleas — Fiction] I. Wood, Don,
1945– ill. II. Title.
PZ7.W846Na 1984   [E]   83-13035
ISBN 0-15-201417-9
Special Edition for Reading's Fun, Ltd.

A B C D E

The original paintings were done in oil on pressed board.
The text is Clearface Roman, set by Thompson Type,
    San Diego, California.
The display type is Clearface Bold, set by Thompson Type,
    San Diego, California.
Separations were made by Heinz Weber, Inc.,
    Los Angeles, California.
Printed and bound by Tien Wah Press, Singapore
This book was printed with soya-based inks on Leykam
    recycled paper, which contains more than 20 percent
    postconsumer waste and has a total recycled content
    of at least 50 percent.
Designed by Dalia Hartman

For Maegerine Thompson Brewer

There is a house,
a napping house,
where everyone is sleeping.

And in that house
there is a bed,
a cozy bed
in a napping house,
where everyone is sleeping.

And on that bed
there is a granny,
a snoring granny
on a cozy bed
in a napping house,
where everyone is sleeping.

And on that granny
there is a child,
a dreaming child
on a snoring granny
on a cozy bed
in a napping house,
where everyone is sleeping.

And on that child
there is a dog,
a dozing dog
on a dreaming child
on a snoring granny
on a cozy bed
in a napping house,
where everyone is sleeping.

And on that dog
there is a cat,
a snoozing cat
on a dozing dog
on a dreaming child
on a snoring granny
on a cozy bed
in a napping house,
where everyone is sleeping.

And on that cat
there is a mouse,
a slumbering mouse
on a snoozing cat
on a dozing dog
on a dreaming child
on a snoring granny
on a cozy bed
in a napping house,
where everyone is sleeping.

And on that mouse
there is a flea. . . .

Can it be?
A wakeful flea
on a slumbering mouse
on a snoozing cat
on a dozing dog
on a dreaming child
on a snoring granny
on a cozy bed
in a napping house,
where everyone is sleeping.

A wakeful flea
who bites the mouse,

who scares the cat,

who claws the dog,

who thumps the child,

who bumps the granny,

who breaks the bed,

in the napping house,
where no one now is sleeping.